Bound

By

Time

A Book

By

April Wood

Copyright 2019

This is a work of fiction. All names, characters, locations and incidents are products of the author's imagination and any resemblance to actual people, places or events is coincidental or fictionalized.

April Wood

Dedication

To my friends and family.

You all stand by me even when I am half crazed and not acting like myself. You inspire the ability to come up with these worlds and I hope you love this one as much as I do.

Chapter One

The color of the midnight sky was something to behold. Abigail stood in the middle of the empty field and leaned back. Her bare feet were digging into the wet ground. She could feel the soil squish between her toes. It was magical. The stars were moving, she knew that. It was obvious to her, but her teacher disagreed. He felt they were stationary, and it was a trick of the eye. She hated to contradict her teacher, but she did anyway.

"Why have you brought me here?" She was swinging her skirt back and forth as she asked. At all times she could sense the song of the earth. It moved her passionately. She often didn't understand her teacher. He was cryptic at best. Her teacher was an old man. He wore his long grey hair in a ponytail. He was fifty years her senior and filthy. She hated being his student, but he was the best.

"Look up, master." She looked over at him. Her blue skirt was dirty on the bottom and her pink blouse was open enough to show the rounds of her breasts. Her long blonde hair was loose and hanging to her waist. She was a beauty for sure.

"Abbey?" The small voice surprised her. By the edge of the wood stood Samuel. He was her little brother and constantly following her. She ran over to him quickly.

"Sammy, you can't be here." She took him in her arms and hugged his small frame. Then she reached out her right hand. "Oscail," she whispered. Then a fold in time appeared in front of her. "Go." She turned him and pushed him through the whole. Then closed her hand. The fold was gone. It had taken her twelve years of study with Hashmere, but she finally mastered it. She was no longer bound by time. Soon she would be her tribe's sorceress and she would become the leader.

"What is keeping you girl?" Hashmere was no longer looking at the sky. He pulled the hood over his head. The robe he wore was old and spoke of his many years in service. Abigail wasn't interested in the old version of anything. This was a new time. She wouldn't be held to the same old rules.

"My apologies, master. I thought I saw something." Abbey walked over to Hashmere. He smiled at her and it made her gag. His teeth were mostly rotten. His smile sickened her. It always meant there was something going on.

"I see your point with the stars. We will enter it in the books. Now can we return to the citadel?"

"Yes, master." Abbey picked up her skirts and walked behind Hashmere. The citadel was only a few hundred feet away. She never looked up from the ground. The path was well worn and safe. When they reached the edge of the citadel the force field started to show. Hashmere stepped up and spoke quietly. A small opening appeared in front of him. They both walked through, and the opening closed.

"Good evening, Abigail." Hashmere bowed and walked off. His movement stunned her. This was a sign of her growing and becoming the new Hesoun. This was the sign she had been waiting to see. Her work had finally won him to her side. She needed his blessing to move on.

She walked the two miles to her home in silence. She simply breathed the air and admired the dew-soaked grass. When she reached the humble dwelling, she found Sammy standing outside. He was pacing and rocking until he caught sight of her. Then he ran headlong into her arms.

"Sissy," he cried.

"Why aren't you in bed?" She held him tight and spun around with him in her arms.

"You didn't tuck me in."

"Oh." She carried him through the doorway and climbed the ladder to the loft. She laid him down on his straw bed and pulled his cover over the top of him. He closed his eyes and she kissed his forehead. She sat down on the ground beside him and stroked his dirty blond hair. He was so little. She was eighteen and he was six. It was just the two of them now. She hummed a few bars of his favorite song. When he was sound asleep, she climbed back down. She spoke a few words and the torches lit up. Then she spoke a few more and the hearth lit up. This little home was all she had ever known. Looking around now she knew it would only be so for a short while longer.

She worried what was going to happen to Sammy. No other Hesoun had children or dependents of any kind. She couldn't leave him alone. He was so young. She sat down in the chair and closed her eyes. Before she knew it, the sun was shining in on her face. She stretched out her body and looked up at the loft. Sammy was still sleeping soundly in his bed.

She stood up and walked to the back room. She grabbed a bucket and headed out the back door. Twenty paces away laid the river. She dipped the bucket in and brought it back to the house. She set some to boil and the rest she put in a wash basin. She quickly washed and stepped into the back room. She put on a fresh blue blouse and blue skirts. Her cinch was tight, but it was the fashion for the day. She never wore shoes, though she owned them. She found being connected to the earth only bolstered her power.

When she emerged, she found Sammy sitting at the table with a bowl of porridge. She had set the water boiling but hadn't gotten out the porridge. Sammy had made it all himself. He was trying to show her how he could take care of himself. It was working.

"Good morning." Abbey sat down and watched Sammy eat.

"Morning." Sammy spoke with a mouthful of porridge.

She turned her hand a few times and then a bowl appeared in front of her. It was filled with fruits. Sammy smiled at her. Then she looked over to the hearth. The water wasn't boiling yet. Then she looked back at him. He smiled and laughed. Then he turned his hand and a bowl of fruit appeared in front of him.

"When did you learn that?"

"Yesterday," he laughed.

"You are watching me closely." She smiled at him. They ate the rest of their breakfast in silence. As they were finishing there was a knock on the door.

"Enter," she said, standing to put the dishes in the basin. She would wash them later if the mood struck her.

"Morning." The deep voice could only belong to one man. Kellan was twenty and a strong warrior for the people. He stood six feet with red hair and green eyes. They had played together since they were children. She had watched him become a man with admiration. He reminded her of her own father. He was strong and steady. Kellan was as familiar to her as her own brother.

"What brings you around?" She asked while still cleaning.

"No patrols this morning. Plus, I wanted to see my girl," he said, stepping behind her and swatting her butt. She jumped and gave him a cross look. He only smiled and winked. Then he sat down and grabbed her bowl. He finished the food she had not. He looked funny to her. He was dressed in black and armed to the teeth. She was dressed in light colors and carried only a dagger at her waist. The irony was not lost on her.

"So. what do you have planned today? No wait, let me guess," Kellan said.

"You know what I have planned today."

"Yeah I know. I got myself assigned to your detail." He chomped down on the last fruit and still looked hungry. She conjured him another bowl of fruit. He smiled at her and dug in.

"Slow down, you'll choke." She laughed and sent Sammy up to his room to change.

"When you are ready," Kellan said.

"What?"

"When you are ready, we will escort you to the citadel for the ritual."

"Oh." She sat down and let it sink in. "What about Sammy?"

"He can come to." Sammy squealed loudly from his room. It startled Abbey. Kellan just laughed along with him.

"Shall we?" Kellan stood and offered his arm to Abbey. She stood and took it as Sammy climbed down. They walked together to the door. Before either of them could reach it, it opened. Standing at her door was a compliment of twenty-five guards. They were all for her. Kellan led her out and down to the path. They walked arms locked down the path toward the citadel. It was an imposing stone building. It was three stories and covered in vines. It had stood for centuries.

As they approached, banners were flung over the sides. They were in her colors and with her crest on them. Kellan was beaming. His body was puffed up in pride. He kept his arm tight on hers. Her other hand was occupied by Sammy.

They came up on the first turret. From the outside it looked as though there would be no way of entering. Kellan let go of her hand as did Sammy. She stepped up to the stone and placed her hands upon it. She let the cold radiate for a minute and then she let her heat spread. Then she blew lightly on the wall and stepped back. It opened up. She took Kellan's hand again and they stepped through. Inside they found a scene only she was prepared for. They were not in the citadel. They were in the woods in the middle of one of the stone ruins. The elders and Hashmere were standing outside the circle. The guards shifted to be near them. That left only Kellan, Sammy and Abbey in the middle.

"Who comes beside the Hesoun?" Hashmere asked.

"Kellan the warrior and Sammy the sprite," Kellan answered.

"And will you remain beside her?"

"We will."

"Then let it all begin."

The area went blacker then night. They could still hear the crowd outside the ring but there was no light to see them. They couldn't even see each other. Kellan still held her left hand and Sammy held her right. This was part of the ultimate test, but it scared her to have them here. She knew what was in store, but they didn't. She wasn't sure Sammy could handle this test. He wasn't fond of the dark on a good day. His hand was tight on hers. She knew he was starting to panic.

"Stay calm, Sammy."

"Yeah little dude. It will be alright," Kellan added.

Abbey felt a smile spread across her face. This test was not going to be easy, but she felt certain they could handle it together. A cold breeze began to blow across their faces. Then the air changed. It was now salty like the ocean was nearby. Then they heard it. The waves were hitting the cliffs with ferocity.

"Abbey, what is that sound?" Sammy was trembling.

"It's the ocean peanut. Don't be scared. This is part of the journey."

"Yeah little dude. It's fine. Just don't take a step forward."

"Okay." He gripped their hands even tighter. Abbey's eyes were starting to adjust to the darkness. Then the light started to come through. It was the early morning. As the tip of the yellow sun crested the horizon they were whisked away again. This time when they stopped, they were high on a mountain top. Each place they were only permitted to see. They couldn't move around or collect anything. This was part of the test. She had to prove that she could take in the information without the use of magic or weaponry. Kellan knew this as well. His hand never left hers or Sammy's. He would not hinder her. He loved her. She grew more aware of this fact the further they traveled. It just felt right. The three of them together was the perfect equation.

Thirty minutes later they were back in the circle. The elders were applauding and chanting her name. Hashmere walked up to her and put his arms around her. Then he bowed to her. The rest of the assembly did the same. It was awe inspiring. Even Kellan knelt down beside her.

"Hesoun!"

"Hesoun, will you marry me?" Kellan asked.

"What?" she cried.

"Will you?"

"Yeah will you sis?" Sammy laughed.

"Yes."

She cried as he held her. The moment was overwhelming for a multitude of reasons. She was now the sorcerer of her people and a leader. It happened in a way that she got to keep her brother and her best friend. She knew she wanted to be with him, but never pressured him. She simply waited for him to make his move and he finally did in a big way. Abbey's heart was so full it was threatening to explode.

Chapter Two

The next morning Abbey woke up not knowing how she got home. The evening had been filled with dancing and wine. She couldn't remember what time it was when the party ended. She felt her head for a moment. She had a slight headache but nothing too severe. Then she sat up quickly in bed. She suddenly remembered she was engaged. Kellan had asked her to marry him. It seemed like a dream until she looked down. There at the foot of her bed lay Kellan. He was still dressed in his uniform. He must have been concerned for her safety.

She stretched and then quietly walked to the river for the morning water. She thought about the last twenty-four hours. Immediately she was swamped with images of her parents. She loved them so much. The tears were flowing so fast she could barely see where she was walking. She sobbed uncontrollably into her skirts.

"Abbey," Kellan cried. His arms were around her in seconds. His strength surrounded her. She put her head on her his shoulder and just wept. He stroked her head and led her back into the house. "You were thinking of your parents again."

"Yes."

"You know that wasn't your fault," he said, helping her to a seat at the table. He took the water and filled the pot. She waved her hand and flame immediately started under it. He sat back down and took her hand.

"Tell me the story."

"Okay. Maybe that will help me."

"I think it will. Just pretend I know nothing and tell me the story."

"It was two years ago. Mother and I had just finished our chores. She was braiding her black hair and staring out the window. Father was due back from his mission at any moment. Mother stood from her chair and walked over to her owl. He was screaming in his cage. He had never done that. It was like he was in pain. Mother tried to calm him, but it was useless. Its red eyes went black and it dropped dead. Mother ripped a portal and took off. I tried to follow her, but I hadn't mastered that yet." Abbey took a break to take a deep breath. Remembering was almost as hard as speaking it.

"When she didn't return, I ran outside. The guard was just coming through the force field. In the back I saw two bodies in a cart. I ran to it. Somehow. I knew it was them. When I saw their bodies lying in the wagon I fell apart. My mother's body was barely marked. My father was covered in blood. I can still remember his black dress and black hair. I buried them and her owl the next day. Ever since, Sammy and I have been alone."

"Not alone." Kellan moved his hand on top of hers.

"Thank you." She bent over and kissed his hand.

"Gross." Sammy was standing by the table. He wasn't amused.

"It's not gross. We love each other. Soon we will be sleeping in the same bed."

"Hopefully the new house will have private rooms," Sammy laughed.

"It will. The next few days will be very full. Kellan and I will marry and then we will all move to the Hesoun home. It is far more protected and much larger."

"Sis, why did they make you Hesoun?" Sammy sat down and conjured some fruit for himself. Abbey snickered before she answered. Then she conjured porridge for Kellan and herself.

"Well, our mother was Hesoun before her death."

"Then why do they call Hashmere Hesoun?" Sammy asked with a mouth full of food.

"Because someone had to take the position until I was trained properly. Hashmere was the same master that trained our mother. He is too old now to keep the position. He can't protect our people."

"Oh. So, because we come from a family of mages, we were the right choice."

"Yes. And someday you may become Hesoun. It will be you or one of my children."

"Our children right," Kellan laughed.

"Yes, my sweet."

"Gross." Sammy laughed again.

Once again, they sat and ate breakfast together like a normal family. This was one of those times Abbey was very happy. She felt her life was more sad than happy, but maybe it was going to change. She had some hope. This was like the past for her. She loved to sit around the table with her family. It was magical. Her mother was a powerful sorceress, but she never gave into the royal life style. She kept them in the simple house and showed them there was more to life than power.

"Shall we?" Kellan asked with his arm out. He was standing in front of her dressed in his full Colonel regalia. She thought he looked sharp indeed. Her thoughts had run away with her and she hadn't noticed him getting up from the table. She took his hand and stood. With the swipe of her hand she was covered in her wedding clothes. Her pink blouse was cinched in by an embroidered corset. The skirts were pink and sheer. They laid in several layers. Each one caught the light in a different way. She turned to look at Sammy. He was in his evening dress one moment and his best suit the next. She really thought he was a marvel. She didn't have that much control over magic at his age.

She flipped her veil over her face and walked out the door with Kellan. Sammy carried her train behind them. When the door opened, she found a compliment of the royal guard standing at full attention. They raised their swords over their heads and smiled as the three of them walked through. At the end of the line Hashmere stood waiting. He was dressed in clean black robes. For the first time in years he looked like the elder he was. He reached out his staff and touched the hem of Abbey's gown. That instant they were teleported to a place deep in the forest. She knew he had set up a force field in advance. It wouldn't do to have the Hesoun attacked on her wedding day.

The place was set up beautifully. There were flowers on everything that stood still. There were ribbons in every color tied on the trees. Hashmere waved his hand and then the trees started to twinkle.

"Please join hands before this assembly."

Abbey took Kellan's hands in hers. Then Hashmere took a long piece of blue ribbon and wrapped their hands together. He held them tightly. Abbey never looked away from Kellan. She felt his love as her own. She knew her parents would have been proud. She wished they could be standing there now.

"This tie binds you together, body, soul, spirit and mind. You will be only for each other. You will live, love and enjoy all things together as one. This union is joined by the gods and the masters of Magdale. No man nor spirit may undo it. So, say we all."

Hashmere untied the ribbon and then flipped up Abbey's veil. Then Kellan leaned forward and kissed her chastely on the lips. She felt a spark of passion deep in her soul.

"Shall we?" Kellan whispered. He took her hand and turned them both.

"What about Sammy?" she whispered back.

"Hashmere, will you keep Sammy for a day or two?"

"Certainly. Enjoy yourselves." Hashmere took Sammy's hand and they were gone. She knew he would be safe, but didn't envy him having to stay with Hashmere. He was not a clean man.

"Where are we going?" Abbey asked.

"I think we should christen every room in our new home," he laughed.

"Good." She took his hand and teleported them to the Hesoun home. She hadn't seen it since she was a child, but she remembered where it was.

Her mother had decorated it in a manner that reminded her of a brothel. It was all dark reds and browns. When the council discovered her father and mother were married and expecting Abbey, they were turned out of the house. She wasn't stripped of her power, but the title was held back. It belonged to their family, but no one had done it married or with children. Abbey looked around the home. It was much larger than her humble place. It was covered in dust. She said a few words and the entire house lit up and became spotless.

"This will do." Kellan walked around the room removing the cloths from the furniture.

"Will it." She winked at him and then ran to the bedroom. Their wedding night was going to be a long, exhausting time.

She ran up the stairs to the master room. She flung her skirts on the ground and removed her blouse. She sat down on the bed and waited for him. He took his time coming to the room. The torture was elegant to her. She shook on the bed. It was scaring her, but she was anxious. When he entered the doorway, he was wearing only his trousers. His sculpted chest made her swallow hard. She waited on the bed for him to come to her. She needed him desperately.

"Are you waiting patiently for me, wife?" He unbuttoned his trousers. Abbey licked her lips and waited for him to come to her.

"I am."

"Good." He walked over to her with the flap of his trousers falling. It didn't reveal anything, but it was tantalizing. He touched her cheek and then took her hand. He pulled her up and spun her around. He moved her hair from her shoulder and started to nibble on it. His hands were roaming over her body. She felt very exposed in her shift and cinch. He kept kissing her neck as he moved to untie her cinch. As each lace let go, she let out a breath. He put his arm around her and let her cinch fall in his arms. Her breasts were now free in her shift. He let the cinch hit the ground so he could caress her.

"Perfect," he whispered in her ear. He spun her back around so he could take a long look at her. He raked her up and down with his eyes. His lust was clear. She was feeling happy about her choice of man. He was control, but soft. It was the right balance for her.

"As are you husband." She leaned over and pulled his trousers the rest of the way down. When his manhood was fully exposed, she was taken aback. It was much more than she had been prepared for. Her virgin body wasn't going to like this intrusion, but she was wishing it.

"Shall we?" He led her to the bed gently. He kissed her passionately as he found his place between her legs. He was slow to enter her. He took his time and moved in inch by inch. She gasped a few times, but she was grateful he did it this way. She wrapped her legs around him when he finally was seated. He rested for a moment, but the want on her face made him move before he meant to. Before long they were pulsing and pushing together in unison. It was as if they had always been destined for each other. It was bliss. They made love all night until her body could take no more.

Chapter Three

"I wouldn't go in there without announcing yourself, lad." Hashmere was trying to spare Sammy any unfortunate views. Sammy was only interested in seeing his sister. Hashmere let out a whistle before Sammy reached the door. He knew what was going on even if the boy didn't.

"Abbey?" Sammy stepped inside and called for his sister.

"In a minute little dude," Kellan called.

He sat down in the parlor and looked around. All the furnishings reminded him of his mother. There were even pictures on the walls of her. He remembered her well, even though he was only four when she died. She was his entire world before that. Now he depended on Abbey. She was more than his sister. She was his mother and father as well. He sat there swinging his legs impatiently waiting.

"Hello, Sammy." Abbey came around the corner. She was wearing her typical blue and pink, but somehow, she had changed. There was a glow about her. He could see it.

"Sis," he replied.

"Are you ready to claim your room?" She lifted her eyebrows and put out her hand for him. He took it and they walked out of the room. She took him up the stairs and let him go free. Their bedroom was at the end of hall. Sammy ran to the second door on the left. He opened it and stood there for a moment. Inside there was a four-poster bed in the middle of the room. It was covered in furs. The walls had some paintings on them. They were brown and tan. Inside there was a door on the left and one on the right. He stepped in and opened the one on the left. It revealed a closet. The door on the right revealed a privy chamber. It was more than he had ever dreamed of.

"Do you like it, little dude?" Kellan stood in the doorway. He smiled and then put his arm around Abbey's waist. He pulled her tight to him.

"I love it, but can I change the color?"

"Sure." Before she even finished speaking Sammy waved his hands and the walls turned blue. It was a lovely deep shade of blue. Then another wave put stars on the walls. It was celestial.

"This is wonderful." He jumped on the bed and covered himself up in furs. Kellan and Abbey laughed loudly.

"There's an old man waiting in the library," Hashmere called out. He was never one for patience. Abbey slid out of Kellan's arms and walked down to the library. Kellan stayed behind to help Sammy get settled.

"Good morning," she said, walking into the room. Hashmere was sitting at the desk looking through the books. He had a way of making himself at home anywhere. He had not lived in this house for forty years, yet he acted like he just left it.

"Hesoun. How are you?" He didn't even look up.

"Well."

"Good."

"Is there a reason for your visit?" She moved toward the desk. He could sense what she wanted and vacated the seat. She took it and then Kellan walked in the room. He sat beside her at the desk. Hashmere took one of the chairs across from it. He was very serious. Whatever he had to say it was weighing on him heavily.

"I am glad you are both here for this concerns us all."

"Go on," she replied.

"The Meridian are moving closer to our northern border. We thought we had them back, but they keep testing. We will need to do something."

"The guard will be ready for whatever you need, Hesoun. We are all ready for action."

"Get your commanders together. We will meet in one hour at the tower." Abbey stood. Kellan ran upstairs. He put his uniform on and hurried out the door.

"I have something to show you," Hashmere said. He took her hand and led her to the back wall. It seemed like a bookshelf, but she knew better. He touched it and spoke some words. Behind the wall lay a small room. In it was an outfit she hadn't seen in years. It was the armor her mother wore. The metal breast plate was fitted with a dragon. It was silver and the dragon was black. There was chain mail on the arms. She put the armor on and then found the weapons on the far wall. There were too many to choose from. She went for the throwing blades and a long dagger. It was all she needed. Then they stepped out of the room.

"Please stay here and watch over Sammy. I don't need him following me."

"I will. Now go. You will need to have the room set up before they arrive."

Abbey ported to the tower. The room was in shambles. The tables were overturned, and it hadn't been cleaned in a while. She spoke the words and the room began to straighten. When it was finished, she spoke an enchantment on the map on the table. It lit up showing the position of their enemies in blue. Their own troops shown in red. The commanders and elders started to trickle in. She greeted them all and waited for her husband's arrival. She knew he would be coming in last. This would be her signal.

When she saw him in his full uniform her knees went weak. She loved this man with every part of her being. She smiled at him and he let her glimpse a small one from him. It was only a seconds' worth but it was all she needed.

"We have a problem," Abbey started. The leaders were all standing around the table staring at the map. She had their attention and would keep it. She picked up her skirts and walked over to the window. "Our enemy is testing our borders. They seek to wipe us out."

"We have had reports of Meridian soldiers on the northern edge of the field," Kellan said.

"Yes. My soldiers have seen them testing it. Throwing stones and such like little children." The commander speaking wasn't familiar to Abbey. She had seen him at the wedding, but still didn't know his name. His laughter pissed her off.

"This is no laughing matter," she snapped. She turned quickly from the window. It made her hair spin in a seductive way. Kellan had a hard time controlling himself. She was stunning. He looked around the table and saw that he wasn't the only one. His smile faded quickly to a growl.

"My apologies, Hesoun. I meant no disrespect. It is simply strange how they go about testing our force field."

"Do you know what will take it down?" She stepped toward him. Her moves were menacing in nature. Kellan noticed her hand was tightly grasping her dagger.

"No, Hesoun. I do not." The commander backed against the table. It moved slightly from the force.

"My death," she whispered in his ear.

"Then we must keep you protected."

"Pray you do. The only reason we weren't lost when my mother died was that she passed her power before her death. I will not be a behind the scenes leader. I will be with you whatever you choose." She was resolute.

"We must set out and attack," Kellan said.

"I agree with Commander Kellan. His company and Commander Jarvis' company should be enough."

"You are suggesting two companies?"

"Yes, Hesoun."

"Hesoun, Commander Reny is right. It will only take two to send a message," Kellan said.

"Commander Reny may be right, but I will not risk my people. I want the camp thoroughly scouted before we send anyone. Do we have scouts we can count on?" Abbey moved closer to the table. It was set up with a few troops, but no one was certain how many there really were.

"I have several men under my command that would do this," Commander Reny admitted.

"Good. Send them now. I want our troops to know what they are getting into. When your scouts return, we will meet again. Commander Kellan and Jarvis will ready their men."

"As you command, Hesoun." All the men bowed and left the room. Abbey stood with her hands on the table. She didn't need to send the scouts. She knew how many there were, but she needed the men to trust her instincts. There were only a thousand troops and very little weaponry. What bothered her was that fact. Why were they there? They came unprepared to take on the citadel. She scanned them until she found the leader. She pulled all her focus and found his mind. He had been trained to keep her out, but she was more powerful than they knew. They knew her mother. They didn't know her. She got passed his defenses and searched his mind for answers.

It was just as she suspected. She was still looking when she felt a hand touch hers. It broke her concentration. She looked to her left to find Sammy staring at her in awe. There was a tear in his eye.

"Why?" he pouted.

"I don't know, peanut."

"Will you stop them?" She bent down and picked him up. She knew he had seen everything she had. She wondered at the connection. She hoped it wasn't a constant, but it did explain a lot.

"That's the plan, peanut." She carried him back into the residence and went in search of Hashmere. She was angry that he let her little brother go.

"He's gone." She put Sammy down and looked at him.

"What do you mean?"

"He's gone, like mom and dad." Sammy was staring at the ground. The reason for his tears was now painfully obvious. She left him standing there and went to the parlor. There in the chair sat Hashmere. He looked peaceful.

"What happened?" She knew Sammy was right behind her. She didn't have to look.

"We were eating and then he just looked at me, spoke a few words and then stopped breathing."

"Was it mage language?" She stepped up to Hashmere and pushed the hair out of his face. She felt very protective of his body. She knew what needed to be done and she would be the one to do it.

"Yes."

"Was today the first time you were able to connect to my thoughts," she asked.

"Yes."

"You bastard," she whispered. She knew what he had done. He passed all his powers onto Samuel. Now Sammy would become powerful at a young age. She was either going to have to train him or send him away. Her decision would have to be soon.

"Don't send me away," Sammy interrupted.

"I don't plan on it, but you know it's not entirely up to me. The elders will decide what is best for you." She put her arm around him and held him tight.

"They won't send me away. I am better when I am with you."

"I hope not, peanut."

"I'm tired."

"Let's get you to bed."

Abbey took his hand and led him to the room. He climbed into bed and she covered him. She kissed his forehead and then went back down to Hashmere's body. She spoke a few words and the body disappeared. She opened a portal and followed him. He was already on the pyre. She started covering his body with bandages. Then other elders came and helped her. They added pieces to his garb and to the fire. They were all things that they associated with Hashmere. When they were finished, she spokc the words and the fire ignited. They all stood and watched as Hashmere's body became ash.

"Hesoun," someone shouted.

"Yes?"

"Hesoun, the scouts have returned." She turned to see a soldier standing there.

"Ten minutes." He saluted and then ran off. He would spread the message to the commanders, and they would all meet. The sun was going down now. It had already been such a long day. A lot was riding on her eighteen-year-old shoulders. Abbey was starting to feel the weight of the world.

Chapter Four

"Abbey," Kellan called.

He had just caught up to her before they entered the war room. He wanted to see if she was okay. He knew about Hashmere but couldn't be there. There was a lot going on right now.

"Husband," she said softly. He put his arm around her waist and pulled her tight to his body. Then he placed a gentle kissed on her forehead. It was a tender moment.

"Are you alright?"

"I have to be."

"I know you do, but you are still my girl. I am concerned." He loosened his grip on her slightly. Others were coming in. He didn't want her to be embarrassed.

"Let's just do this," she said.

They walked into the room together but separated almost immediately. Abbey went to the window and Kellan took his place at the table. The scouts had already informed the leaders, but Abbey had more to add. She waited for them to finish discussing their plans. They had it all figured out. The two companies would march and then destroy the small group encamped on the northern border. It was a sound plan, but it wasn't going to happen. She knew that.

"Your military prowess becomes you Commander Reny. However, there is more to this equation than just what meets the eye." She never turned and faced them. Instead she stared out the window toward the strangers. She wished with all her heart things could be different, but they wouldn't be. She had to do what was coming next. Her family and indeed her people depended on her. The Versade race needed to continue.

"You have other plans, Hesoun." Reny's tone was condescending. She would normally reproach him for that, but Kellan beat her to it.

"You don't talk to the Hesoun in that manner. She is our leader. Show her some respect!" He slammed his fist down on the table. It made her jump, but she was proud of him.

"My apologies."

"Forgiven." She still never turned to face them. The weight of the world was on her and she felt it more now than she had ever felt in her life.

"Have you a plan, Hesoun?" Commander Jarvis asked. She finally looked in his direction. Jarvis was a handsome man. His six-foot frame was large and imposing, but his gentle blue eyes spoke of his sincerity. He wore his blond hair short. It was the fashion for officers to keep it clean cut. The younger men wore theirs in ponytails like Hashmere. He had started the fad without even trying. Her mood turned sorrowful thinking of him. She felt his loss with every step she took.

"I have a plan Commander Jarvis. It doesn't include the use of troops. It requires the sacrifice of one person."

"Sacrifice?" Reny was annoyed when he spoke.

"Yes. I need one brave soul to infiltrate the camp and drop my gift in the middle. I have no hope of this person returning. Though it could be possible."

They all looked at each other. What she said was serious. She was asking for one of their soldiers to give up their life for the good of the people. She could see it wasn't sitting well with them. She didn't expect this to be easy. Her penetration of the leader had revealed the truth. She had to be the one to end this conflict before it had a chance to begin.

"I have read the mind of the leader. If we attack them it will cost us. He is there as a decoy. His leader has sent him so they may gauge what kind of attack we will use on them. Then they will use our policies and procedures against us." She paced the floor. The sigh she let out let everyone in the room know how serious this was to her. She wasn't playing a game or even acting impulsively. She had given this much thought and worry. It wasn't easy for her to ask someone to sacrifice like this. It was hard, much harder than an eighteen-year-old should have to manage.

"I have just the person. And I think he can make it out," Jarvis said. He stood only five foot ten inches. His hands were on his hips like he meant business. His jet-black hair was starting to sport white streaks. He was nearly forty now. For a soldier that was considered old.

"Good. Have him here after the moon is at its peak. I will have the package ready for him. Please instruct him to place it in the cauldron and run back. If he is fast enough, he will make it back to the force field without injury. If not, I will give him a quick death I promise." She took his hand and he kissed hers. He bolted out of the room. The rest of the commanders bowed and walked out. They were discussing things as they left. Kellan stayed behind. He stood with his hands on the table just staring at her.

"Are you going to be okay with this?" He was sincere. He stood up and walked over to her. He put his arms around her and squeezed.

"I have to be. There is no other option. I won't have you out there as guinea pigs for the Meridians. We are Versade. We are proud and we will not be their pawns." He saw a few tears in her eyes. There was really nothing he could do to help her. This was her battle. She had to fight it alone. He knew that. It didn't make it any easier. He kissed her cheek and then left the room.

"So, what are we creating?" Sammy was excited. He took her hand and walked her to the window. They both looked at their enemies. The sun was down. Now they were obvious with their fires.

"We are building a poison. It has to be fast and work in water." She cleared the table with one move of her hands. Then she called forth the ingredients. There was a candle on the table. Sammy lit it by blowing. This was the source of heat they would need to finish the concoction. She started putting ingredients in the mortar. She used the pestle to crush and combine them. It was dangerous work, but she had been trained well.

She moved the items into a vial and added some liquid. Sammy did his part by chanting the entire time. It was to protect her from the ingredients. Then she put the vial over the flame. It started as a green color and then changed to yellow. Then she sealed it with a cork. Sammy placed his hand on it and spelled the vial. This way it should explode on impact with water. As they finished Commander Jarvis appeared at the door. Next to him was a short boy. He had long black hair and was tiny in every way. Abbey thought for sure he might make it back, but his size would help her end him quickly.

"Hesoun, this is Bakeer. He will be your runner." Jarvis pushed him forward slightly. She could see this boy was overwhelmed by meeting the Hesoun in person. It was a rare treat.

"Bakeer, please rise."

"Hesoun," he replied, bowing.

"Please take this vial and drop it in the cauldron in the center of the encampment. You will have five minutes to make it back out and to the force field. If you do not make it there, I will end you before the poison can. I would not wish that on any of my people."

"I will make it, Hesoun." He took the vial and bolted out the door. Abbey had some hope, but not enough. The events of the last twenty four hours had made her more cenacle then before. She knew her parents would be unhappy with her current train of thought, but she couldn't stop it. It was just too much for her. She bowed to Jarvis and went back to the window. She used her magic to watch the events unfold.

Bakeer scouted the camp for a moment or two. He was looking for the best way to get in. When he found it, he ran quickly to the cauldron. Most of the encampment were sleeping. He had gone undetected until just before reaching his target. The man tried to raise the alarm, but Bakeer was trained well. He slit the man's throat before a syllable could escape. He rushed to the target and dropped the vial. Sammy was chanting in the corner of the room. A thick fog started to form at the cauldron.

Abbey watched with a lump in her throat. Bakeer ran steadily back toward the field. Before he could reach the edge, Abbey saw the fog nipping at his heels. She decided she couldn't let him fall, not after his show of bravery. She folded the time right in front of him. He instantly teleported into the room and ran right into Jarvis. He knocked him to the ground. Jarvis was angry and then relieved. He had been certain when he sent him out it would be the last time, he saw the soldier.

"You did your people proud, Bakeer." Abbey didn't turn around. She was busy watching the poison do its work. The men were falling in droves. It sickened her and excited her at the same time. She knew tonight would be crazy with her husband.

"You didn't have to do that, Hesoun. Thank you." He was out of breath but grateful. The fog was seconds away from taking his life. It would have been a waste for sure.

"Thank you for your assistance," Abbey said. She was trying to be gracious.

Abbey decided to take the rest of the night off. She was going to show her husband some much needed attention. If they were lucky, they might get a few hours of sleep. She needed it for sure.

Chapter Five

The small hand touching hers wasn't her husbands. She knew before she ever opened her eyes Sammy was sitting on her bed. He was quiet enough. She didn't even feel his weight on the bed until she was fully awake. He was very talented. She was aware.

"What's the matter, peanut?"

"I couldn't sleep." He laid down beside her and snuggled into her arm. She let go of his hand and stroked his hair. It was her way of comforting him. She knew their mother had done it since he was a baby. When she passed, Abbey just continued the tradition.

"I know."

"Will it stop?" She had the same nightmares when she finally fell asleep. Death was going to be a part of their lives. They would both have to embrace it entirely.

"I think it will get easier, but it won't stop. You will always see them. We have to understand it was something we had to do. Now I need to get up. The elders want to discuss you today," she said, kissing his forehead.

"Don't let them send me away." There was a tear in the corner of his eye. She would do what she could, but ultimately it was up to them. She was afraid they were going to be driven by their fear. Sammy was stronger than any other mage in their kingdom. She knew that in her soul. He was the future of her line. Her children would be just as powerful as Sammy, if not more.

"I will do what I can." She conjured a dress and then wrapped her hair up. It was pretty but didn't take much effort to do. She always did more than a braid for the elders. It was a sign of respect.

"I know," he said. He slid off the bed and conjured an outfit. She was impressed with his choice, but it was fitting. He would be called in to talk to them.

He took her hand and they closed their eyes. Just like that they were teleported to the ruins. This was where the elders always met. It was tradition and would not be changed. Sammy held her hand tightly. Kellan wanted to be here for this, but the generals were out patrolling the border lands. They were destined to be going in opposite directions.

"You know why you were summoned, Hesoun?" The voice was coming from Elder Johns though they couldn't see him. The ruins were dark. Abbey would recognize his voice anywhere, though.

"I do, Elder Johns."

"What is your suggestion then?"

"I suggest he stay with me until he is of proper age. Then we can discuss outside training."

"And what is the proper age?"

"I believe ten to be the right age." Sammy squeezed her hand tightly. He wasn't happy with the age, but she knew she had to give them something realistic. If she started too high the meeting might end abruptly.

It went silent for ten minutes. She knew they were communicating telepathically. She could have interrupted their conversation, but she wouldn't let them know how powerful she was. It was bad enough they were afraid of her little brother. She wouldn't give them anymore ammunition.

"We agree to your terms, but he will be sent away to train when he is ten."

"Thank you. I understand your instructions and will follow them."

"We trust that you will teach him well. When he is sent out, we want him to represent us well."

"He will." She took his hand and squeezed. Then they were gone. They reappeared in her bedroom.

"Was that good?" Sammy immediately changed into his more comfortable clothes. He hated to dress in mage costume. It was confining.

"It was. You will stay here with me for four more years."

"Then what?" He jumped on her bed and bounced a couple of times. She sat down beside him and brushed his hair out of his eyes.

"Then you will go away to Mage school as I did."

"Did you like it?"

"Do I have to be honest?"

"Yes."

"Then no. It is harder for us. We are full blood mage. The strength in our heritage is more than most have seen. That can create jealousy and other problems. But you are a boy. It may not be as difficult for you as it was for me."

"How will I live without you?" He laid his head on her shoulder.

"You won't be without me. You will just be further away." She stroked his hair. She would not lose him for any reason. The school was a must, but she could keep an eye on him even while he was there. Her baby brother was in fact her first baby. The one growing in her womb would be the second. She hoped he would think of the baby as a sibling and not as a niece or nephew.

"Why do you worry about the baby and me so much?"

"I just want things to work out. Why are you reading my mind?"

"It was loud. I couldn't resist. Don't worry, this baby is my sister or brother," he said, rubbing her belly gently.

"Thank you, peanut."

"What's going on in here?" Kellan's deep voice echoed off the walls.

"Just saying hi to my sibling," Sammy said, with a smile plastered on his face. Then he jumped up and walked out of the room.

"Sibling? Did you forget to tell me something?" Kellan's eyes were sparkling as he looked at his wife.

"Well," she said, getting up from the bed and walking toward him in the doorway. "You are going to be a father." He pulled her into his body with his strong arms.

"What?"

"I'm going to have a baby."

"How do you know?" he whispered in her ear.

"I'm a mage sweetheart. I would know."

"Are you sure?"

"If I wasn't Sammy just confirmed it for me," she laughed.

"I love you," he whispered and then kissed her neck.

"I love you too."

Chapter Six

"You know what we have done will only keep them at bay for so long. Sooner or later they will figure out we used magic to get rid of them." Kellan was pacing back and forth in front of her.

Abbey finished dressing. She knew how serious this was. They had gotten rid of the early threat, but there would be more. There were always battles amongst the tribes of this Island. It was almost bred into them. If you were with one tribe you hated the others. It was as simple as that. It wasn't simple for Abbey. She had sympathy for them. They were not a bad people. The Meridiens were just trying to make it in this world. She knew they had a sorcerer of their own, but he would not even half compare to her. She also knew they were the ones responsible for her parents' deaths.

"I know you worry, but you needn't." She threw her shawl over her shoulder and walked out of the bedroom. Her bare feet enjoyed the cold stone in the morning. It was unusual, but Abbey loved being connected.

"I will worry every day of my life because it suits me," he said, running up behind her and swatting her but. She gave him her best don't do that look and joined Sammy in the kitchen. He was already dressed and inhaling his breakfast.

"So, what will we learning today?" He was far too excited for her liking. She knew how to curb that.

"We will be looking into the archives and studying spells." She sat down at the table and conjured Kellan and her breakfast. She smiled as she saw

Sammy start to pout. She was going to do something else with him today. She had to really work hard to keep it out of her mind. She didn't want to give it away too early.

"Fine." Sammy got up and walked to the library.

"You shouldn't tease him, so." Kellan laughed as he finished his porridge.

"It's fun for me. I will take him out to the old house and teach him spells. I want him ready for the school. Those kids are mean."

"You think he will need to protect himself?"

"Yes. They will try to break him because of the power he wields. They did the same to me. It's just jealousy. Since I only have a few years I will get him as prepared as I can." She finished her breakfast, kissed Kellan and found Sammy reading in the library.

"How's it going?" She walked over to the couch he was on. He had one of the thickest books in the room. He was trying his best to study it.

"Good, I guess." She almost laughed at the disappointment in his voice. She had to put him out of his misery.

"Come." She took the book out of his hands. She closed it and sent it back to wear it belonged.

"Where are we going?" He jumped up and took her hand.

"You will see." She closed her eyes and spoke a few words. The next minute they were standing in front of the house they used to call home. "We will be practicing some defensive spells." She conjured two attackers and stepped away from Sammy. She knew she was throwing him at the deep end of the pool, but she had to see where he was.

She stood and watched as he never backed down once. He stood his ground even when one of them landed a punch. He stood strong and threw as many spells as he could. It made her heart feel lighter. She knew he wouldn't be pushed around by the other kids at the school. Now she was thinking he might go sooner. He was so powerful. He needed to learn how to control it. She couldn't teach him all the things they could. It was something she would have to talk with him about later. It should be his decision.

He dropped the last attacker with ease. "How did I do?" he asked, completely out of breath.

"You did really well, peanut."

"So why do you want to send me away." He sat down on the grass and played with the clovers. She came over and sat beside him.

"Only because I want you to learn everything you can."

"I will learn what I need from you and what has to be done from them. You need to keep me here until the time is up. Otherwise I will miss out on important information that may save my life one day." She looked at her brother. He was in earnest. He didn't want to leave but she knew he would when it was time. It made her want to cry. He was so much like their father. He too was strong and knew every step he had to take. It was an intuition. Their family was highly gifted on both sides.

"I will do as instructed by the council. I hope you know you are one of the most impressive sorcerers I have ever known. You are going to do big things." She patted him on the leg and then conjured a picnic basket. He wasted no time. There was an apple in his mouth within seconds. She laughed at him and grabbed a sandwich for herself. They ate quietly for a while. The sun was high but not hot this time of the year. It was cool and there would be frost soon.

"Shall we go back and read?" Sammy stood up and waited for her.

"I think we should. Which book did you have in mind?" She stood up and brushed off her skirts. She took his hand and they were in the library in seconds.

"I want to read the old one I had." He called the book off the shelf and sat down.

"What's so impressive about that book?" She fell on the couch beside him.

"It's got a lot of important information. It speaks of mistakes made in the past. It also speaks of the future." Sammy started flipping pages and reading to himself. She watched him for a moment. He was cute curled up. He was taking each page seriously. Some he even stopped to read twice. He was well on track to out do her in most things. She got up and started to pace. She was thinking about their enemy. Then Kellan walked in the door. His face expressed why she was suddenly thinking of them.

"What's happened?"

"We've had a reply from the King of Meridia."

"And?" She was on her toes feeling anxious about what this could mean. They didn't need a war. She was conflicted inside.

"He wants blood."

"What does he know?"

Kellan took a moment to answer. She could tell he didn't want to say what was on his mind. "He knows magic was used. He doesn't accuse you. He thinks someone else did it and wants their blood. Otherwise it will be war."

"Well war it is." She was angry now. She called her battle armor quickly. She walked out of the room and right to the war room. She was going to put an end to this if it meant ending every Meridien there was. She sent out the birds and waited for them to arrive.

"What are you doing, love?" Kellan walked over to her and touched her hand.

"We are going to ride out to meet them. We can't keep doing this. There has to be resolution even if it means war."

"I think there is wisdom in your crazy, but should we be so rash?"

"He sent spies to keep an eye on us. Not to mention how many people he has killed. I will meet this King on the battlefield. I won't cower."

"That's what we want to hear." The room was suddenly filled with all the generals. She was impressed how quickly they had responded to her.

"I want to take two legions of soldiers and meet this King. He will know my fire and will answer for his crimes before I answer for mine."

"I think we can support this action." The glimmer of evil in Jarvis' eyes gave her pause. He had lost family members needlessly as well.

"Good. I think we can manage with Jarvis and Kellan. I want to leave within the hour. I am sending birds to him now. He will know we are coming so that we may meet him properly." She conjured a bird and let it fly. It would take only minutes for it to reach its target. The men made some plans and then left the turret. They would have to gather the troops and make the necessary arrangements. She was excited at the thought of it. This would be her first battle. The men had seen skirmishes before, but she had not fought anyone. Her mind was busy trying to figure it all out. This was going to be the making point of her leadership role.

Chapter Seven

"I wish I could come with you, sis." Sammy held her hand as he walked with her to the horse. She was wearing black armor with pink blouse and black britches. It would not be good to walk into battle in a dress.

"You are yet too young to fight for the clan. I will allow you to view through me as long as it doesn't interfere."

"Thank you." She climbed on the horse and he walked back to the house. He was sad to see her go, but he knew she was right.

"Let's go." She kicked her horse and took off. The two legions followed her. Kellan and Jarvis were by her side. She knew they would wait on her unless she made a mistake. She had no intention of making a mistake. She felt how important this was for her status in the clan. It would solidify her leadership role.

"Hesoun, will we wait by the shield as the troops pass through." Jarvis was asking a logical question. She had not even thought that far. They would have to wait there as she was the only one that could close it.

"Yes, commander. We will wait until the last person comes through." They rode the rest of the way to the shield in silence. She rode her horse up and whispered, "Oscail." A section of the shield lifted easily.

Kellan went through first and waited just on the other side. Abbey took up a place beside him and Jarvis waited on the other side. It took a few minutes for all of the soldiers to pass through. It was tedious, but it kept the people she loved safe. She closed the shield and the three commanders rode fast to get ahead of the column. When they reached the front, she felt something stir with in her. She knew the King was nearby.

"Halt." She put up her fist and waited for a moment.

"What are we doing?" Jarvis asked.

"I can feel him nearby. We must send out scouts, so we are not caught off guard."

Kellan found the men he trusted the most and set them out. Then he moved the entire company off the road. If the King was out there, they could be ambushed on the road. It was safer for them to wait in the tree line. Abbey watched him as he took control. He was confidant and smooth. She loved him dearly, but now she respected him. She saw it had taken him time to win the trust of these men. He had done it. She felt her heart skip a beat. She would give her very life for him. It was this moment that showed her what happened to her parents. They died for each other, trying to protect each other. It was moving to think of. She couldn't cry in front of this company but she really wanted to. She climbed down off her horse into Kellan's arms.

"Are you alright love?" He asked her so quietly she was surprised she heard it.

"Yes. Just figured out a personal truth."

"Good." He led her back into the trees. When they were out of the line of sight of the men, he kissed her on the cheek. It was passionate. She knew her man wanted to comfort her anyway he could. He would even take her here if it would improve her spirit. She knew she was very lucky.

"It shouldn't take them long to find something. They will report to us here." Kellan helped her down to the ground. Jarvis was already sitting under a tree chewing on a stick. He was very cool and calm. They were on the verge of a battle and he looked like he was waiting for tea. She admired his strength in the moment. He was a rock. It was refreshing. They sat there in silence for about ten minutes before the scouts returned.

"Commander!" The young man rushed up to them as Kellan helped her off the ground.

"You have news?" Abbey didn't wait for either of the men to answer. This was her expedition. She wanted to know first.

"Hesoun," the kid dropped to his knee and bowed. "The King is nearly here. He has about two legions of men with him. There is also an old man accompanying him. They are headed this direction with haste." He stayed on the ground. She put her hands on her hips and paced for a moment.

"We have the surprise in this situation. We should leave half of the men hidden in the trees. The other half will form on the road. We will meet him head on. I will need one of you to stay here and lead the attack if there needs to be one."

"It will be my honor." Jarvis was quick to volunteer and even quicker to get his men in position. She casted her hand over the trees. When they stepped onto the road, they could no longer see Jarvis and his men. Her illusion was very successful. She prayed it would hold until they were needed. She mounted her horse and headed toward the King with Kellan at her side. She was nervous but she wouldn't show anyone. They rode for only ten minutes. Then they could see the King coming up the road. What took her breath away was his age and the fact one of her teachers was beside him.

"Halt." The company stopped behind her. She looked at Kellan. He knew she wanted him to go with her. She didn't have to ask. He was in tune to her needs on every level.

They strode to the other company slowly and with purpose. She chanted the entire way. She would have her old teacher bond. She wouldn't allow him to use anything on her. She tapped into Sammy to help her. He was watching. He knew what she needed. He pushed her spell harder. She felt the charge of his energy. She looked directly at him as their spell wove over him completely. He was useless. She smiled knowing he would be helpless.

"Abigail, what a lovely surprise." The King spoke with an elegance she hadn't expected. He sat on his horse in silver armor and a gold crown on his head. His hear was jet black as was his beard. He wasn't an ugly man. She had hoped he would be old.

"I haven't had the pleasure." She stopped her horse just barely in front of his.

"I am King Jonah. This is the road to Meridia. What can we do for you?" He looked over at the old man. Abbey suddenly remember his name was Ignatious. The look they shared let her know they knew she had done something. She smiled.

"Well King Jonah, I am Abigail of Veridia. I am the Hesoun to my people. This is commander Kellan. We have come in answer to threats of violence."

The King looked at her for a moment before he decided to answer. She saw he was calculating. This was going to cost him. She was sure of it. "If my sorcerer is right you caused great harm to a company of men I had camped on the boarder. This would be enough for me to attack if war was what I wanted."

"I don't know how your decrepit sorcerer would know anything." She was taunting him. She wanted him to try his powers. It would hurt immensely. For his part, her old teacher remained still. He knew what it would do to him. She wanted him to suffer. He picked the wrong side of this to be on.

"He is gifted when he is not under your spell." Jonah smiled at her. It wasn't wicked. It was a knowing smile. She was intrigue. She felt his ability to charm was strong, but she wasn't easily tricked by anyone. Even without her powers she was cunning. She would show him this.

"If you know what I have done then why have you not attacked?"

"My advisors have advised against it. They say there is a sorted past between us. Now how can that be true?" He was in earnest or so it appeared. There was something lying just beneath the surface. She couldn't break her concentration long enough to find out. She had to answer him with nothing but honesty.

"My parents were murdered by your people."

"That can't be true. I have only been King for a year, but I think something of that magnitude would have been told to me. At the very least there should have been rumors of it."

"I can't answer that." She shifted in her saddle uncomfortably. Something bad was stirring. She could feel it. He wasn't what he seemed. She sent a message to Jarvis to prepare for an attack. It wasn't a moment later when she heard it.

"What the hell?" Kellan was angry. He made the distance to the Kings side in seconds. He had his sword to the King's throat. He moved fast when there was something going on.

"I don't know what is happening. My men are all behind me as you see." He was eerily calm with the blade at his throat. Kellan was facing him on his horse. She rode to the side of him and touched his hand. She knew she could because Kellan would kill him if he moved. She felt his intention and saw the truth. She had to shut Sammy out. The images moved through her with a violence she had never experienced. She didn't really want to see what he was showing her, but it was too late now. The information was a part of her and always would be. She would live with this forever. He wouldn't help her remain calm. She got closer to him. She moved her mouth right up to his ear.

"I know the truth. You will suffer for what you have done." She moved her hand quickly and tied him up with magic. She bound the sorcerer in the next move. With the leaders in her hands Kellan took no time to act.

"Take them out!" Kellan was in the throws of it immediately. His men followed him headlong into battle. It was a glorious sight to behold. She was enthralled watching them tear Jonah's men apart. They left no man standing. Jarvis came out of the woods just in time to kill the stragglers. The men were covered in blood and wore out. She took her prize. She held him in the air behind her as they rode back to the citadel. It was a high she couldn't describe. It made her feel sexual. She would be strong with Kellan this evening. Now they needed to imprison the two men responsible for her parents' death. She would have to comfort Sammy. She knew he had seen the truth. He was going to need to process it as much as she did.

Chapter Eight

"Let me at him!" Sammy was screaming as he came down the stairs. He looked ferocious. For eight he was tall and lanky. It was like an octopus was running down the stairs. He was all legs and arms.

"That's enough, peanut." Abbey grabbed him before he could get by her. When Jonah started screaming, she knew he was casting. She spun him around and sent him back up to the house with a spell of her own. She locked his door hoping he would get the hint. She could hear him still screaming on the other side of the door. She couldn't deal with him right now. There would be lots of questions that had to be answered. Her action was bold.

"Take him to the dungeon. Maybe my brother won't be able to get to him there." She looked Jonah right in the eye. She wanted him to know her baby brother was punishing him. It made her want to laugh, but she dared not encourage Sammy. Without his sorcerer the King was vulnerable to any attack. Sammy was strong but not stronger than her, yet.

The guards took the prisoners down to the dungeon. She went right to the war room. There would need to be explanations given. When she arrived, the leaders were already around the table. There was a general feeling of malice in the room. She knew they wouldn't understand. It didn't matter. They would soon enough. She wasn't going to cater to anyone. She was anointed to her position. They would have to respect her choices.

"Before anyone has a reason to explode let me explain. I read this King. He was merely a soldier when my parents were killed, by him. He became the ruler by this act. He was proud of what he had done. There is no mercy nor pity in the man."

The room fell silent. She wasn't sure what to say next. Her only intention was to get as much information as she could from him. She knew Sammy had more planned for the King. She wasn't sure what would happen if they did put him to death. The leadership might want retribution, or they may be grateful he was gone. It was in the air for her. She would have to really focus to get the answers.

"Hesoun speaks the truth. I knew this man when he was a soldier. He was there the day her parents were murdered. I can't say I saw him do it, but it is likely. Especially since they promoted him so fast." Jarvis was standing on the other side of the room. He was still wiping blood from his face and blade.

"We took out two legions of their men this day. They will not have the strength to come against us for some time. Whatever you decide to do with him, Hesoun was right. He was treacherous and had evil plans." Kellan stood beside her confidently. He was every bit the commander just now. She would hold onto this image of him for tonight. It would keep their play time very focused. She shook her head. Others knew how to read minds. She needed to keep her mind on the present.

"I don't know what you wish to do with him. I know what Sammy wishes for him."

"What do you sense in the air?" The kindly man standing in front of her was named Marcus. He was nearly sixty and had been a leader for a long time. She found him to be very patient with her. His gray hair and green eyes made her feel peaceful.

"Right now, it is very confused. This could be coming from me, but I rather think it is coming from them. A good majority didn't want this man as King. He had no familial rights nor was he high born. They have tolerated him out of fear. He was propped up to this position by the sorcerer Ivan."

"What?" Marcus was shocked by her news.

"He is in the dungeon with Jonah."

"How did he come to such a pass? He was always the best teacher. I believe even you had him."

She waited for a moment. She didn't want to share the evil things in her past, but they needed to know this one. She looked at Kellan. "Ivan stole something very precious from me. Something I could never get back."

Kellan took her hand and smiled at her. He was giving her permission to say it. “Ivan raped me while I was at the school.”

“What?” Marcus was genuinely surprised. He looked at her with nothing but shock and concern.

“He did this to many of the younger kids. It was part of his initiation to the school. There is a lot that goes on at the school that would shock most of you. I won’t go into to it, but he was already corrupt.” Kellan squeezed her hand and took his place next to the other commanders. The room fell silent. She walked over to her seat at the head of the table.

“I don’t know what the solution is gentleman. We need to come to a consensus. For mine and my brothers’ part, we want him killed slowly.” She sat down and waited for the debate to begin.

"I know I wish this as well," Marcus replied. There were twelve other people at the table. They would respectfully voice their opinions one at a time. Everyone agreed with one exception. Allain sat to her right. He was only three years older than her. His position was inherited a few months ago. His father died a sudden death. The circumstances were questionable. She wanted to read him, but she would need to touch him. He looked at her with his brown eyes sparkling. His short brown hair was neat, and he looked every bit the lord.

"I'm not convinced this man needs to suffer a brutal death. So far all you have accused him of is killing two people I didn't really know." His tone offended her. It offended her baby as well. It was now moving the fluid in her belly. It shouldn't be able to do that, but she knew the baby was strong and very magical. It shouldn't even have a conscience yet. She rubbed her belly to calm it down.

"He killed the hesoun and the general of the armies. This is enough for me." Marcus answered before she had a chance.

"Okay. So, this means we are going to draw and quarter him, disembowel him and then hang him."

"Not in that order, but yes." She felt good answering him.

"I just don't see what this solves."

"It solves having an enemy out there." Marcus was frustrated. He got up from the table and started pacing the room.

"We do things by consensus. It is important we are all on the same page. It will happen with or without you. It would be better for our people if you agreed." She looked right at him. She wanted to reach out and touch him, but they would all know why she wanted to do this. It would be obvious, and she couldn't afford to alienate anyone. They were all on her side right now. Any high jinx and that could change.

"Well that puts me in my place." Allain feigned being offended. She saw this was an act.

"I am not putting you in your place, Allain. I simply stating we all agree this needs to be done. I am sorry if it puts you out. That is not the intention." She almost touched his hand. Kellan shot her a look just in time.

"I will agree to this if there is clear evidence of my objection registered." The scribe looked over at him and nodded. His hand was moving just as fast as it could. Allain looked back to her. "You have my consent. Now when will this take place and who will do it?"

"I would like for this to take place at dawn. As for executioner, the lords present should choose."

"I think either Jarvis or Kellan should have the pleasure. They are both skilled and could manage. It was also their men that suffered." Marcus stood up and then sat down. Abbey looked over to Kellan. She didn't want him to be the one. She knew he could do it, but she didn't want him to.

"I will take the King and Kellan can take care of the rapist." Jarvis smiled at his decision. He knew Kellan was itching to do something to the man. It was in his nature.

"Hesoun should be there keeping Ivan in control." Allain looked at her and smiled. She couldn't tell whether he was happy to suggest for a good reason or bad one. This man was an enigma to her.

"I can handle these suggestions. Then the prisoners will be brought to the square at dawn. I want their body parts set out on our borders. I think this will be enough." She stood up and smacked the table. "Until tomorrow." Kellan walked over to her and they walked back to the hesoun house together. When she opened Sammy's door, she found him curled up in a ball on the floor. His face was stained with tears. Kellan picked him up and put him in the bed.

"Are we going to kill him?" Sammy whispered.

"Yes, love."

"Good." She kissed his forehead and he went right back to sleeping.

Kellan took her hand and pulled her out the door. She shut it and followed him to their bedroom. When she walked through the door, she found him naked in the middle of the room. "I know your looks love. You have been dreaming of this all day."

She pulled the armor off her body and then pulled her cinch. She dropped her gown on the floor and stood before him. "I can't help watching my husband slay all those men turned me on." She smiled and walked to the bed. She climbed on and laid on her back. He spun around fast and walked over to the bed. He stood there admiring her body for a while. Occasionally he would lick his lips. She found that irresistible.

"Are you going to join me, or should I get started on my own?" She playfully ran her hand down her body. She stopped just shy of the curls. He was nearly drooling. He waited a few more seconds than joined her on the bed. He got between her legs and started kissing her breasts. She wrapped her legs around him eager to feel him inside of her. He didn't make her wait long. He was as eager as she was. He moved slow to begin with it. She wasn't feeling that patient. She flipped them over, so she was on top. This way she could control the speed. Right now, she was wanting fast and furious. She was tired and didn't want to waste any time. She rocked hard on him. He just let her go. She was moving with such ferocity they were both going to explode in minutes.

"Kellan!" She screamed with a violence he wasn't ready for. The room was full of soldiers with in seconds. He grabbed the blankets and covered her quickly as she collapsed on his chest. She was laughing.

"We are fine. Get out and close the door."

"Yes, commander."

He lifted up the blanket to find her fast asleep on his chest. He gently removed himself from her and placed her on the bed. He covered her and went to the bathroom. When he came back, he sat on the bed and stared at her for a while. She was lovely as she slept. He knew he would do anything for her. She was the entire world to him and would always be.

Chapter Nine

The morning broke red and bloody. It was fitting for what they had planned. Abbey opened her eyes. Kellan was dressed and ready to go. She knew she had overslept. She conjured her pink blouse and skirts and then her cinch. She threw her hair up in braids. He took her hand and they met Sammy in the hall.

"You sure you want to go little man?"

"I'm sure." Sammy was definitive. He wasn't about to miss out on this most important day to our family. It took some convincing, but he didn't leave her alone until she said yes. Of course, he did this all telepathically. This was why Abbey overslept. Her brother was being very persistent. He didn't care she was pregnant and worn out.

"You will remain quiet and not try to help." Abbey was sure she could manage him. He wasn't going to do anything but witness the event. There was no need for him to help at all.

They walked to the square as a family. Kellan had put on his hood just outside the door. His identity was supposed to remain hidden. As was Jarvis'. When they reached the platform, a small crowd had already gathered. There were people walking into the square even as they set up. Jarvis and Kellan went up the stairs and examined the tools that had been brought out for them to use. They were both looking them over very carefully. Kellan even sharpened a few of them.

"Sammy, stand here with Marcus. He will keep you safe." Sammy stood by the man. He didn't want to, but he wasn't going to push his luck. He knew she didn't really want him here and could send him away at any moment. She climbed the stairs. She couldn't help but look at the instruments laid out. They were intimidating. She knew what they were all used for but had no desire to use them. She thought, perhaps, that would change when Jonah was on the cross. The first thing they would do is stretch them. Then they would be disemboweled. The last thing was drawn and quartered. This was done with heavy horses. They were hitched to the side of the platform.

She looked around. All the leaders were present. She looked over to the guard. "Bring out the prisoners." He nodded and then walked to the dungeon. A few minutes later Ivan appeared at the door. He was chained at the hands and feet. She knew he could do damage even like that. She cast a bonding spell over him. She looked down to Sammy. He was chanting as well. She knew he would want to help. She should be angry, but he was adding to her power. Ivan wouldn't be able to break this spell. Right behind him was Jonah. The smile on his face gave her pause. She hadn't wanted to play his game, but it seemed she was. She could do nothing to stop it now.

They were led through the crowd of people. The commoners threw rotten fruit at the prisoners. The spat on them and yelled obscenities. When they reached the platform, she directed Jonah to Jarvis and Ivan to Kellan. She hoped he would do his part well. She knew he had rage towards this man. She was certain he could rip him a part with his bare hands.

"These men have been accused of murder. They stand before you guilty. On this day they will meet their gods." Abbey spoke forcefully. No one would oppose her. She knew that. She nodded to Jarvis and Kellan. They put a noose around the neck of the men and pulled. It stretched and choked them but wasn't enough to kill. It was merely meant to cause pain and get the men to confess. They tighten and loosened the rope several times. There were clear red marks around their throats. Neither man was at a point of speaking. She gave Kellan a nod and then Jarvis. They took the men down and put them on the cross. The shackles on their hands and feet were placed into a locking apparatus. Their hands were stretched out over the heads. The set up pulled them tight, but not too tight. Kellan walked over to his instruments. He picked up a long bladed first. He stepped up to Ivan and put two cuts in his cheeks. They weren't deep, but they bled. The man laid there silent with blood dripping down his neck. Jarvis went next. He was crueler. He took Jonah's left ear first and then his right. Then he leaned down to the whole.

"I know you can still hear me, pig. You would do well to confess your sins. Then I might have mercy on you." Jonah said nothing. He simply spit at Jarvis. Jarvis laughed.

Kellan put the blade back and grabbed a thinner blade. He started on Ivan's left arm. He made small slashes starting at the wrist and working his way down to the arm pit. None of them were deep enough to end his life, but they were painful. "You know how to make this end. I can be merciful. You need only confess."

There were tears in Ivan's eyes. He wasn't as defiant as Jonah. "What would you like me to confess to?"

"All the evil you have done. Meet your maker with a clear conscience." Abbey looked Ivan. She had to make sure he was still bound. She wasn't sure if he would confess yet or not.

"If you will stop this torture and kill me mercifully, I will confess."

"I will get on with your disembowelment and then you will be drawn and quartered." Kellan stepped back. They were hoping he was being serious and that he would give them what they wanted. Closure was what everyone present needed.

"Fine. In my years at the school I raped nearly fifty students. I punished hundreds that didn't deserve it. I joined forces with Jonah. We plotted to kill your Hesoun and her mate. With their deaths Jonah was able to rise to the level of general and then King. We both killed the previous King so this plan could happen."

"Is this all your soul wishes to release?" Abbey stood over him. She wanted him to know she was the one responsible for his end. No one else but her.

"Yes. Now please end this for me."

Kellan took out the curved blade. He moved with force and speed. He cut open Ivan's belly and pulled out his intestines. Ivan had tears rolling down his cheek, but he made no sound. When Abbey was happy with his work, Kellan unhooked his shackles. The guards carried him over to where the horses were waiting. They hooked him up to the horses. On a nod from Abbey the soldiers hit the horses so they would go. It took only seconds for them to pull Ivan's body apart. It was gruesome. Several people in the crowd lost their lunches. His pain was now over.

"Jonah, have you anything to say?" Abbey stood over him. He was bloody.

"I have nothing to say to you."

"Please continue." She stepped back and watched Jarvis work. He took the same thin blade Kellan had used. He was making slashes up and down Jonah's legs. Jonah cried out in pain several times but would admit nothing. Jarvis grabbed the curved tool. It took minutes for him to empty the contents of Jonah's gut. Jarvis reveled in his work. He made it look like art. It was brutal and beautiful.

"Hesoun, this man is unrepentant. I believe it is time."

"Thank you. I believe you are correct."

That was all he needed to hear. They unhooked Jonah and carried him to the horses. When they attached him, the ground was still bloody with Ivan. Jonah said nothing. The order was given, and the horses pulled with all their might. It took three good pulls for them to succeed. That scene was even more gruesome than Ivan. It was hard to even look in that direction. Kellan took off his hood and took her hand. He walked back to the house with her hand in his. She said nothing. Sammy followed behind as quiet as they were. It seemed the day had been dramatic on all of them. It was fulfilling and devastating all in the same breath. It was more than any of them ever thought they would go through. This day would stay with them all forever.

Chapter Ten

She woke with the sun streaming in on her face. The warmth felt like a kiss from her mother. She knew she would have been proud of her. The day before had been horrific and long. They were out there with Jonah and Ivan for six hours. It was time consuming and unpleasant. She hoped there would be no fallout from it. They didn't send the body parts to Meridia. They could have. She felt this was the wrong course of action. So, she decided to put them along the border of their land as a warning to others.

"Morning, wife." Kellan kissed her on the cheek. She opened an eye and watched him walk out of the room. He was ready for the day. She wasn't even awake yet. His stamina impressed her. She knew he was strong when they were just children. He out matched every guy in their class. His ability to strategize was obvious from about eight years old. She thought she loved him from that time. He was her hero always. She decided to get out of bed. Today wasn't going to be particularly hard, but she would need to help Sammy through it. As she sat up, he came running into the room and jumped on her bed.

"Hey, peanut." She brushed the hair out of his eyes as he sat down in front of her.

"So, what are we learning today?" It was as if yesterday never happened. She was impressed and a little scared.

"I am not sure. Is there something you want to learn?"

"I would like to look at our family lineage."

"Any particular reason for that?" She yawned and stretched her arms above her head.

"I have a theory, but I want to look at the details. Is that okay?" Sammy was being earnest with her. She didn't need to push him. He would tell her the truth in time.

"Okay. Now let me get dressed and I will meet you in the library." He smiled and ran out of the room quickly. She went to her privy and washed her face. Then she dressed in her pink shift, skirts and corset. When she made it to the library, Sammy was already on the floor thumbing through the lineage books. He was very intent on the pages. She knew he was looking for something specific.

"Is there something I can help you with, peanut?" She sat down on the floor beside her brother. She loved getting down to his level. She knew she wouldn't be able to for much longer. The baby inside her was growing rapidly. Her corset was already too snug on her.

"Look right here." He pointed to the middle of the page. "Mother kept these records about her cycles."

"You know what that means?"

"Yes. I can't say I like knowing, but I do know."

"Okay, so she kept records."

"She also kept records of what she calls unions." Abbey's face went scarlet. She knew she was going to have to tell him sometime, but she was hoping for a few more years to go by.

"Unions are when her and father would lay together." She said it as quickly as she could manage.

"Gross." He stuck out his tongue and made a gagging noise. At least he wasn't growing up too fast. She laughed at his gestures.

"So, is there something there?"

"Yes. I did the math. Mother said she carried me for five months. She said this was normal for powerful sorceress. According to this math, dad wasn't my father." He pointed to the information on the page. Abbey leaned in and read it. She did the math as well.

"Hmm. She never said anything to me." Abbey was trying to process it. Her mother told her a lot. Now she really wanted to know what was going on. There was really only one way to find out.

"We will have to call her." Sammy was sitting on his knees looking at Abbey. She was thinking about the spell and what it would take to call her mother from beyond.

"It will have to wait until tomorrow night. We need the pull of a full moon to help us."

"What are we doing tomorrow night?" Kellan asked, walking into the library.

"We are calling mother." Sammy was pointing to himself and Abbey.

"Kellan can help us."

"If you say so, sis. I'm going to gather some of the herbs we need." Sammy jumped up and left the room.

"What was that about?" Kellan put out his hand and helped Abbey off the floor.

"He has some issues from yesterday. Most of them revolve around the fact he didn't get to help kill anyone." They walked over to the desk and put the books on it.

"Oh. I guess that makes sense. So, I should just give the little dude some space."

"I think that will be best. Any news?" She took his hand and walked out of the library with him.

"There has been no news, which is good. I would rather hear nothing than hear there is an army headed our way." Kellan lifted her hand and kissed it.

"Good. I wanted to take this day to myself. There is a lot that needs to be done around the house."

"I need to get back to my legion. I want to run them through the gauntlet this afternoon."

"Has anyone ever beat your time?" She smiled at him. She was genuinely proud of her soldier.

"No and they never will." He laughed and kissed her cheek. He left her in the hall and went back to the training grounds. Now she was alone she wanted to change the décor of the house. It was her mother's taste and not hers. She started where she stood. She made the dark wood floors cherry in color and smooth. The walls were green and now they were brown. She put some of Sammy's artwork on the walls in frames. She made them look as good as she could. She wanted him to be very proud when he saw them.

She left Sammy and her bedrooms alone. They were great. Sammy had been so unique with his choices she wouldn't dream of taking them away from him. Her bedroom was already her taste. It was the one room in the house her mother hadn't made gaudy. The entry way was red with gold trim. Abbey changed it to brown with pink trim. Pink was her signature color. She always wore it. Unless she was in battle, then black was the color of the day. When she was finished it was time to lay down. She made her way to the bedroom and found Kellan already soundly sleeping. She knew immediately he had joined his soldiers in the gauntlet. She kissed his cheek and stripped down to her shift. She laid down next to him. Tomorrow night was going to be hard on her. It would take all her strength to call her mother. They needed to get to the truth of the matter if they could. Sammy would always be her brother, but it was important to know who his father was. It could explain a lot about him.

Chapter Eleven

The next day went by much slower than she had wanted it too. There were several herbs she had to forage for, and she had to make the candles. "Do we need this one?" Sammy was running around like a crazed little boy. She wasn't upset by it. It was quite distracting. They were walking along the edge of the woods. They were in the force field. She felt uneasy today. She wasn't sure if it was because of what they were doing, or if there was something on the horizon. Until they got this done, she wouldn't be able to focus much.

"No. The one just to the left. It's white and purple. Make sure you don't crush it." She was being very maternal, but these herbs were poisonous. She wouldn't want her brother sick for any reason.

"I know, sis." He pinched the plant off below the danger line and ran back to her. He placed it in her basket delicately. She smiled at him and let him run ahead again. There were about twelve more herbs and flowers for them to find. It was time consuming. Sammy had found six last night. It was a great head start.

"Right there, peanut. The red one." She pointed to the plant beside him. He looked at for a moment. When she reached him, she saw why he wasn't acting. On the other side of the forcefield was Ivan's head. Sammy squatted down and looked at the dead eyes of the man responsible for raping Abbey. She tried to read him, but he put up a wall very fast. She knew he was improving, but this even impressed her. It took her a full year to master that one.

Sammy studied the head for a while and then went back to picking like nothing had happened.

"How many do we need?"

"We need five flowers from this one and three from the one next to it."

"Good. Now we are almost done." They moved away from the gruesome scene. She was happy to be away from it. Her stomach wasn't good right now.

"Just down in the next valley we should find the rest of what we need. Then we need to stop and pick up a large vat of tallow on the way back."

"Do we need to pick up some wicks as well?" Sammy skipped as they moved down the hill. Abbey was focusing on not falling. It wasn't steep but the morning had left a lot of dew on the grass.

"We might need some. We are going to make a dozen candles with this mix."

"I think mom's old hanger is still in the house. Should I grab that?"

"We have one in the new house. It will work just fine."

"Will you let me dip this time?" Sammy stopped and faced her. The look on his face almost made her laugh. He was so serious. Of course, there was a reason he was asking. She had made candles after her parents were gone. He had asked to help. They were nearly finished with the task when he dropped the entire hanger on the ground ruining all the candles. He also got burned in the process.

"I will. You aren't a little boy anymore. I will let you do whatever I can. You need to learn." She smiled as warmly as she could at him. She loved her brother with all her heart. He was her pride and joy.

"Good." He ran ahead of her. "How about this one?" He was pointing at a green plant on the ground. She moved quicker. There were so many bad plants in this area. He was smart, but she often had to cast to find out which was which.

"No, no." She waved her hand over it. It shone bright white.

"Oh. So, this cast." He waved his hand over the flower next to the green plant. It didn't light up at all.

"That is exactly it. Before you pick anything do this. It will save you sickness and in some cases death."

They walked through the valley practicing the new spell. They found all the herbs long before they were done. She let him try it as many times as he wanted to. Mastery of the craft took practice. This was the biggest lesson to learn. Patience wasn't something you came by naturally when you came by conjuring. It was always instant gratification. The very first lesson they taught at the school was learning to wait. It was hard for every student to master.

"We should head back, peanut."

"Okay. You head to the house and I will get the tallow."

"Can you handle it?"

"Yes," he said, running toward the citadel. He was nearly there when she finally crested the hill. He would probably beat her home, but she wasn't in a hurry. They had to wait for moonrise anyway. It was several hours away.

When she walked through the door, she could smell the tallow already cooking. She couldn't get mad at him. She knew he was as excited to talk with their mother as she was. He shouldn't have been cooking alone. When she got to the kitchen, she found him with

Kellan. Her heart was instantly lightened. She never wanted him cooking alone. He wasn't a baby anymore, but she didn't want to risk him.

"So, what are you fellas doing?" She kissed Kellan on the cheek and handed the herbs to Sammy. He started sorting them immediately.

"We are getting these ready to hang." He tied the last string on the hanger. It was ready to dip in the tallow. Kellan dipped it one time and let it hang over the cauldron. The wick would dry allowing them to make several layers.

"Let me cut those, peanut." She stepped over beside Sammy. She took the knife off her belt and started separating leaves from stems. She knew from experience which ones could be crushed and which ones couldn't. She made very quick work of it. She spun around and dropped them all in the cauldron. She spoke some ancient words and the tallow turned green. She smiled at Sammy. He was mesmerized by her.

"Is that the color we need?" Kellan checked the hanger to see if the wicks were dry.

"Nearly. Give it three more minutes. The green should be paler."

"I will go get the blankets." Sammy ran out of the room quickly.

"Is he going to be able to handle this." Kellan waited for her to nod her head. He was holding the hanger like it wasn't heavy. She knew she wouldn't have held it that long. Her arm would be shaking terribly. She smiled at him and nodded. He dipped the candles in for the first three times. Then Sammy came back into the room.

"I get to help." He ran over to Kellan and stepped up on chair. Kellan let him hold as much of the weight as Sammy could handle. They dipped the candles six more times.

"That's good." Kellan moved the candles to the table. Abbey spelled each one as she cut them from the hanger. Sammy laid them gently in a bag. It was quite the family endeavor. Abbey looked outside. It was dark. The moon was finally rising. It would take them thirty minutes to get to the sight she wanted to use. It would work out just right. She grabbed her cloak and covered her head. Kellan took her hand and they all walked out toward the woods. She kept them headed in the same direction for nearly twenty minutes. Then she turned to the left. Before them was a valley. It had very few trees and lots of grass. It was a place her mother frequented. It was the right place. She felt connected to her mother already.

"Right down here!" Sammy was in the middle of the grass throwing the blankets down. He was excited. She knew this was going to be difficult on both of them. Hurting Sammy was not what she wanted, but this was going to hurt no matter what she did.

"Kellan set the bag down in the center, please." She touched his arm and smiled. He kissed her on the cheek and did as she asked.

"Where do you want me, sis?"

"Find a blanket, sit and chant." He ran right to the one in front of the bag Kellan sat down. He immediately started chanting.

"Where would you like me?"

"If you wouldn't mind the out side of the blanket circle."

She walked into the center and sat down beside the bag. She spoke a few words and candles leapt out of the bag. They placed themselves in circle just outside of the blankets. She spoke two more words and the candles were lit. She sat there breathing deeply for a few moments. She felt Sammy's power infusing her. It was time.

"Mother, we have come here tonight to speak with you. Please come forward." She heard Sammy chanting then the air went fully silent. She opened her eyes. She could see no one around her. There were no blankets, no Sammy, no Kellan. She stood up. In the distance she could make out a figure slowly heading toward her. The red hair was the only clue she needed.

"Mother?"

"Daughter." Gwen walked forward in long white gown and cape. She looked angelic to Abbey. It was fitting.

"How are you?" Abbey wanted to kick herself for asking. It was just a natural thing to ask.

"I think death becomes me." She smiled and embraced her daughter. Abbey fought back the tears.

"It does."

"So, why have you asked me to come forward?"

"I don't know how much you know from your side."

"I know you are pregnant with my first grandchild. I know you killed my murderer. Am I caught up enough?" Gwen looked at her daughter and then placed her hand on her belly. The baby did her best to let her know she felt it.

"I guess you know everything." Abbey laughed. It started out genuine and then became fake. She felt it.

"That means there is more. Please sit." Gwen took her hand off Abbey's belly and gestured to the ground. The two women sat. It was silent for a moment.

"We need to know who Sammy's dad is. He is far more powerful than he should be. We checked your records and we know it isn't father."

"You are right, it isn't. I didn't write the name in the book because the experience wasn't one I wanted to remember." Gwen looked at the ground. Abbey saw the pain was intense on her mother's face.

"I didn't want to do this, mother. There has been too much going on. Finding Ivan with the King was a shock to me. He was a horrible person, but he was always a neutral teacher. Now I just want to get to the entire truth. Jonah had help. I think knowing who Sammy's father is might help me get the answers I am seeking."

"I know you want the truth, but it isn't time. There will be. I can't give it to you now."

"Then what do you suggest?"

"I suggest you keep on the path you are on. Everything will reveal itself when it is time. I know it isn't what you wanted but it is all I can give. Now I will bring Sammy over and then you must go back."

Abbey closed her eyes and then opened them. She was back in the circle. Kellan stood outside the blanket ring with his back turned. Sammy was no longer on the blanket. She knew she had to remain in her position. Sammy needed to see his mother. She wouldn't give him the information either. She knew once Gwen's mind was made up, it was made up. There would be no changing it. She looked over to his blanket again. One moment he wasn't there the next he was. He had tears in his eyes, but he looked happy. She casted a spell and all the blankets were packed. The candles burnt down quickly. She touched Kellan on the shoulder. He spun around and kissed her. She was already crying. He picked her up and carried her home. Sammy stayed beside him quietly crying as well. It had been emotional but not for the reasons she had expected. She knew now she could summon her mother anytime. It would be invaluable to her later. She knew that. She felt bound by time now. She couldn't go forward nor could she go back. She was stuck in this place and there was no exit for her. She would need to find a way out of it in order for her family to succeed. There was a way out, but where it was unknown. She would keep searching until her brother and her were free.

About April Wood

I began writing at the tender age of 12. It started with just poetry and then in 2008 I wrote my first full length manuscript. Ever since I have been writing as often as I can. We moved to Missouri 2016 and have loved it. I am also a disabled veteran.

Don't forget to support your favorite authors by giving reviews.

Other books by this author

(The Mist Series)

Outside the Mists of Time

Beyond the Mists of Time

*

(Enticing Series)

Enticing

Endless

Tempestuous

(Stand Alones)

For the Love of an Angel

Passion's Potential

It happened in a Dream

(The Cast Series)

Blood Cast

Wind Cast

Stone Cast

Fire Cast

*

(Dale Series)

Bound in Mirendale

Grown in Gorendale (March 2015)

*

(Changes Series)

A Vampire's Eyes

Vampire's Breath

Vampire's Blood

Vampire's Love

Vampire's Strength

(Co-Author works)

w/Elizabeth St. John

Tempted by Fairies

Washed up, A Merman's Tale

Country Strong

Lover's Bound

Contact this author

Email: apejaywood@yahoo.com

Twitter:

https://twitter.com/apejaywood

Facebook:

https://www.facebook.com/authoraprilwood

Web page:

http://www.aprilwoodauthor.com

57621523R00088

Made in the USA
Columbia, SC
12 May 2019